Story by Carla Mooney

Illustrated by Kathleen Spale

Samson's Tale

To North Riverside
Public Library,

Kathleen Spale
5/25/11

Story Pie Press | Virginia

Publisher's Cataloging-in-Publication

(Provided by Quality Books, Inc.)

Mooney, Carla, 1970-
    Samson's tale / by Carla Mooney ; illustrated by
Kathleen Spale.
    p. cm.
    SUMMARY: Daniel, a young boy, is diagnosed with
leukemia, and his loyal and loving golden retriever,
Samson, sticks by him through all the ups and downs.
    Audience: Ages 4-8.
    LCCN 2010938216
    ISBN-13: 978-0-9842178-2-3
    ISBN-10: 0-9842178-2-7

    1. Leukemia--Juvenile fiction. 2. Dogs--Juvenile
fiction. 3. Loyalty--Juvenile fiction. [1. Leukemia--
Fiction. 2. Cancer--Fiction. 3. Dogs--Fiction.
4. Pets--Fiction. 8. Loyalty--Fiction.   I. Spale,
Kathleen, ill. II. Title.

PZ7.M7792Sam 2010   [E]
          QBI10-600207

Published by Story Pie Press
Copyright 2011 Story Pie Press, LLC
All rights reserved.
To request permission to reproduce selections from this
book, email **publisher@storypiepress.com**.

www.storypiepress.com

Edited by Mary Rand Hess

Book design by Amber Leberman

The text of this book is set in Adobe Garamond Pro.
Other typefaces used are Adobe Onyx MT
and Adobe Myriad Pro.
The illustrations are done in mixed media.

Printed in the United States of America

To my hero, Daniel James, who amazes me with his strength and courage every day. — C.M.

With much love to my family and friends, especially Eric, Sue, Cale, Magan, Brian, Annie, and Ruby (the wonder dog). — K.S.

Samson thumped his tail against the porch steps. *Thump. Whump. Thump.* Today, Daniel was coming home. *Thump. Whump. Thump.*

Daniel had never left Samson
for so long. While Daniel was
away, no one played ball with
Samson. No one took him for
long walks
to the park.

Samson heard Daniel's mom and dad talking about "leukemia" and "hospitals." He didn't know what those words meant. He only knew that while Daniel had been gone, no one smiled.

Thump. Whump. Thump.

A car pulled into the driveway. Samson raced down the porch steps. His tail whipped back and forth like a windshield wiper.

"Shoo, Samson." Daniel's mom pushed him away from the car. "Give Daniel some space." Samson whined. Why couldn't he jump and lick Daniel's face like he always did?

Daniel stepped out of the car. "Samson!"
Samson ran into Daniel's open arms. "I've missed you,"
Daniel said. He rubbed Samson's ears. "I wish you
could have been at the hospital with me."

Samson followed Daniel into the house, up the stairs, and into his bedroom. Was it bedtime already? "Let Daniel rest, Samson," his mom said. "You can play tomorrow." Samson curled up on the floor next to Daniel's bed. He would rest, too.

The next morning, Daniel's mom brought in a tray
of juice and little white pills. "Yuck." Daniel stuck
out his tongue. "I hate taking medicine." "I know,"
his mom said. "But it's helping you get better."
As she turned her head away from Daniel, Samson
saw her eyes were wet.

Daniel patted the bed and Samson jumped next to him. Daniel buried his face in Samson's furry coat. "The doctors say I have a cancer in my blood. It's called leukemia. I have to have a lot of shots and medicine called chemotherapy to help me get better. I can't even go to school for a while."

He hugged Samson tighter. "I wish I never got sick," he whispered. Samson licked and nuzzled Daniel's face. Daniel was still his boy, cancer or not.

There were many days when Daniel went to the doctor. Samson always waited at the door until Daniel came home. He wished he could go to the hospital, too. He'd have to figure out his own way to help Daniel.

Thump. Whump. Thump.

Sometimes, chemotherapy made Daniel tired.
On those days, Samson kept watch over him.
Other times, medicine called steroids made
Daniel very hungry. Samson helped him clean up
the kitchen. Even when chemotherapy gave Daniel
a stomach ache, Samson found a way to help.

Samson also learned to walk close when Daniel's legs
wobbled. It felt good when Daniel leaned on him.

One afternoon, Daniel's mom shaved off his hair. "It was falling out anyway," said Daniel. Daniel's dad shaved his head, too. Daniel laughed when Samson licked his smooth head.

On Daniel's first day back to school, Samson walked with him to the bus stop. "What if the kids make fun of me?" Daniel asked. Samson rubbed his head against Daniel's leg. He didn't think a new haircut or big words like leukemia and chemotherapy changed Daniel. "Thanks, Samson," Daniel said.

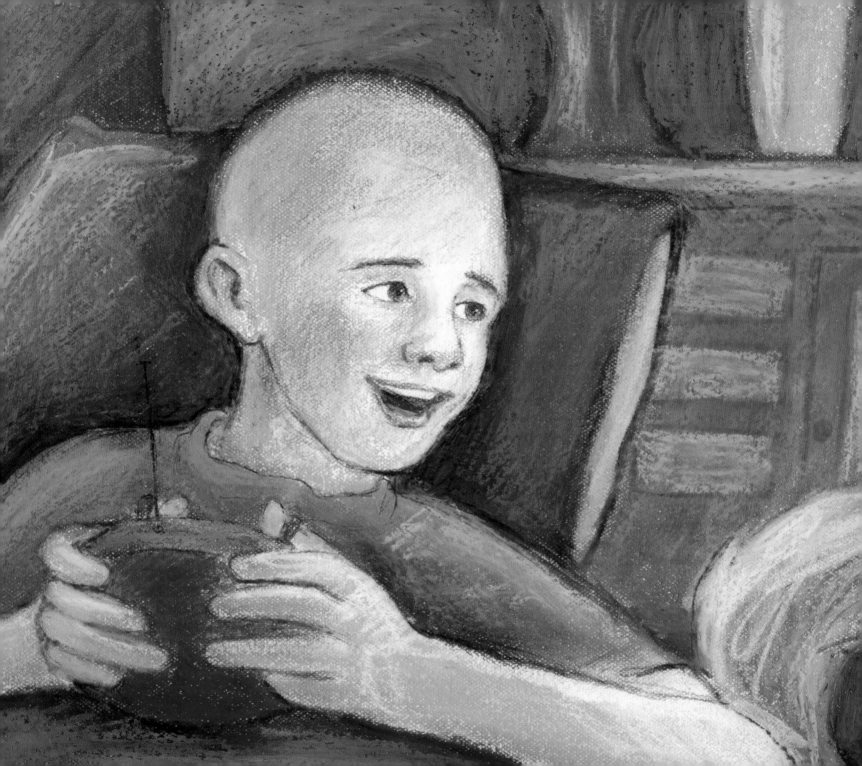

In between doctor visits and medicine, there was still
time to play. Some days, Daniel felt strong and threw
the ball for Samson to catch. But when Daniel's
medicine made his arms and legs ache,
they played catch in a different way.

After a while, Daniel's hair grew back. His walks with Samson grew longer and longer.

One day, Daniel's mom and dad invited all of their family and friends over to the house for a big party. "Our hero," they called Daniel.

Daniel leaned close to Samson and hugged him. "You're *my* hero," he said. Samson wagged his tail.

Thump. Whump. Thump.

Carla Mooney

is the author of more than 20 books for kids and teens. *Samson's Tale* is her first picture book for children. As long as she can remember, she has been in love with reading and writing. She is thrilled to create adventures and explore new worlds in each of her books and hopes readers enjoy the journey as much as she has. Carla lives near Pittsburgh, Pennsylvania with her husband and three children. When not reading and writing, Carla volunteers as the Pittsburgh Chapter Director for Flashes of Hope, a nonprofit organization that photographs children with cancer and other life-threatening conditions. Learn more about Carla and her work at **www.carlamooney.com**.

Kathleen Spale,

a graduate of Academy of Art University in San Francisco, has loved drawing and painting for as long as she can remember. Over the years, she has created artwork for everything from gallery shows to personal commissions, although her greatest passion is creating artwork for children's books. When not illustrating, Kathleen resides and works as a librarian near Chicago. Please visit her website, **www.kathleenspale.com**.

Story Pie Press'

books are made from the heart. Like a great pie, each book is filled with only the finest ingredients. Our mission is to publish books that will entertain and delight, support our children, and help raise awareness for causes related to health and education. The topping: each book is associated with a charitable cause, supporting the organizations that care about the future. Our motto is "heart-filled and good for the soul, creating stories that will have a positive impact on the lives of our young readers, the organizations and charities we support, and the world around us." We're proud of what we're baking here at Story Pie Press. Visit us online at **www.storypiepress.com**.